ROSEMARY WELLS
Max's Chocolate Chicken

Dial Books for Young Readers

NEW YORK

For Janet, who helped enormously

Published by Dial Books for Young Readers
A Division of Penguin Books USA Inc.
375 Hudson Street
New York, New York 10014

Printed in the U.S.A.
Design by Atha Tehon
First Edition
(b)
3 5 7 9 10 8 6 4

Library of Congress Cataloging in Publication Data
Wells, Rosemary. Max's chocolate chicken.
Summary: When Max goes on an egg hunt with his
sister Ruby, he finds everything but Easter eggs.
[1. Easter eggs—Fiction. 2. Easter—Fiction. 3. Rabbits—Fiction]
I. Title.
PZ7.W46843Masj 1989   [E]   88-14954
ISBN 0-8037-0585-9
ISBN 0-8037-0586-7 (lib. bdg.)

The full-color artwork for each picture consists of
a black ink drawing and a watercolor wash.

One morning somebody put
a chocolate chicken in the birdbath.

I love you! said Max.

Wait, Max, said Max's sister, Ruby.
First we go on an egg hunt.
If you find the most eggs, then you
get the chocolate chicken.

And if I find the most eggs, then I
get the chocolate chicken, said Ruby.

Max went looking for eggs,
but all he found was a mud puddle.

Ruby found a big yellow egg.
Max didn't find any.
No eggs, no chicken, Max, said Ruby.

Max went looking again,
but all he found were acorns.

Ruby found a blue egg.
Max, said Ruby, pull yourself together.
Otherwise you'll never get the chocolate chicken.

So Max went looking with Ruby.
Ruby found a red egg with green stars.
Max found a spoon.

Ruby found a gold egg with purple stripes
and a turquoise egg with silver swirls and
a lavender egg with orange polka dots.
Max found some ants.

Then he made ant-and-acorn pancakes.
Max, said Ruby, you'd have trouble
finding your own ears if they weren't
attached to your head.

Ruby counted her eggs.
I'm the one who's going to get the
chocolate chicken, Max, said Ruby.

But Max ran away.

And hid.

The birdbath was empty.

Where are you, Max? Ruby called.
Max ate the chicken's tail.

I see you, Max! said Ruby.
But she didn't.
Max ate the chicken's head.

I'll give you half the chocolate
chicken, Max! yelled Ruby.
Max ate the wings.

Then he popped out of his hiding place.

I love you! said Max.